The Unwanted Puppy

The Unwanted Puppy

by Holly Webb

Illustrated by Sophy Williams

tiger tales

5 River Road, Suite 128, Wilton, CT 06897
Published in the United States 2019
Originally published in Great Britain 2018
by the Little Tiger Group
Text copyright © 2018 Holly Webb
Illustrations copyright © 2018 Sophy Williams
Author photograph copyright Nigel Bird
ISBN-13: 978-1-68010-449-3
ISBN-10: 1-68010-449-7
Printed in China
STP/1800/0257/0219
All rights reserved
10 9 8 7 6 5 4 3 2 1

For more insight and activities, visit us at www.tigertalesbooks.com

Contents

For Zoe and Zach, Lucy and Georgia

Chapter One
The Discovery

Jade wandered along behind her dad, looking for daisies in the grass. She wanted the ones with the wide stalks and pink-tipped petals to make into a bracelet. There were just a few starting to open up now that spring was coming.

She was gazing so closely at the grass around her feet that she was almost nose to nose with the dog before she saw it. She stopped, half crouching, staring into a curious, furry face. Jade loved dogs, and she thought she was good at recognizing what kind they were—she had a huge dog breed poster on her wall. But she didn't know this one.

It had thick, soft fur that was mostly black on its head, but with a white muzzle going into a white stripe up its forehead. There was a splash of orange-brown on the sides of its muzzle, and it had the most beautiful orange eyebrows. They stood out against its black fur and made it look very surprised to see her. Its ears were fluffy and long, like a spaniel's. Though it definitely wasn't a spaniel,

Jade was sure.

Even though the dog was big, Jade thought it must be a puppy. It had that teddy-bear look—cuddly and big-legged, as though it hadn't yet grown into its paws.

It was beautiful.

"Hello, sweetheart...," Jade whispered, wondering if the puppy was a boy or a girl. She eyed the puppy sideways, trying not to stare too much into its eyes and scare it. Her old dog, Honey, hadn't minded—she even liked being hugged, which a lot of dogs didn't, but she had known Jade forever.

The puppy leaned forward—and licked Jade's cheek, making her giggle. Without even thinking, she reached out and rubbed one of its fluffy black ears. Then she stared at it guiltily. She loved dogs, but her mom and dad had made her promise never to pet one without asking the owner if it was okay first. Not all dogs were as friendly as they looked, so it was always best to ask. Jade hadn't meant to break her promise, it was just that this cute puppy had licked her....

"You're beautiful," she whispered. "I wish I could play with you! I'm sure you *are* friendly. Where's your owner, hmm?"

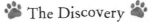

She looked around. The puppy's leash was tied to the playground fence, so maybe it belonged to one of the families who were playing inside. The playground was busy, though, just after school pick-up time, and Jade wasn't sure who had brought the puppy.

"Jade!" Her dad waved from the gate. "Come on!"

Jade sighed and smiled at the puppy. "Bye, beautiful! Maybe I'll see you again sometime," she added.

"Did you see that cute dog?" she asked her dad as she ran up to him. "Look, over there by the fence."

"Wow. Very cute," her dad agreed.

"I don't know what kind of dog it is," Jade said thoughtfully. "But I think it's a large breed—it's really big already,

and I think it's still a puppy."

"I don't know, either." Her dad looked back over his shoulder. "Do you really think it's a puppy?"

"Yes! Well … probably." Jade sighed and slipped her hand into her dad's, leaning her head against his arm. "I miss Honey."

"Me, too." Her dad sighed. "That dog reminds me of her a little—I think it's the fluffy ears."

"Hers were even fluffier," Jade said loyally. "She was the best dog ever."

Honey had died in the autumn the year before, and Jade had been devastated. Her parents had owned the gentle golden retriever before Jade was born, so she'd never known their house without her. She still woke up

some mornings and forgot that Honey wouldn't be there when she went downstairs, sniffing and licking and loving her, all one giant wag.

"She was," her dad agreed. He was silent for a moment as they came through the park gate and out onto the road, just a little way down from their house. "Maybe we'll have another golden retriever one day," he suggested. "I bet you'd enjoy having a puppy."

Jade looked up at him in surprise. After Honey had died, Dad had said he didn't want to think about having another dog, not yet. She tried to imagine a different golden retriever lying in Honey's favorite spot, next to the kitchen radiator. It was difficult—the new dog looked just like Honey.

Still…. A puppy…! Jade smiled to herself, thinking of walks with a dog again and curling up to read a book with a loving dog's nose in her lap. "Yeah … maybe…."

Bear turned to watch the girl walking away from the playground, his tail still wagging faintly. Was she going to come back? He had liked her petting his ears and paying attention to him. He let out a hopeful whine, standing up to peer farther around the fence. But she was gone.

The puppy heaved a sigh and slumped down, stretching out his big tan and white forepaws and resting his muzzle on them. He wished Jack would hurry up and come and play with him. It wasn't much fun sitting here. He could hear baby Tina wailing and he sat up again, looking worriedly into the playground. Jack was on the top of the jungle gym, and Tina was in the stroller, with her mom leaning over to comfort her. Everything was all right....

Still, he stayed watching, ears pricked a little. Tina's crying made him feel anxious, as if he should be doing something to help her, but he didn't know what. Jack was coming back across the playground now, looking grumpy. They were about to go home, Bear realized, wagging his tail so hard that it smacked against the bars of the fence.

Jack came hurrying over to pet him and untie his leash. Bear bounced around his feet, whining and jumping excitedly, while Jack giggled. As Jack and Tina's mom came out of the playground gate, Jack called, "Can Bear pull me?"

Bear looked around curiously as Jack picked up his scooter, which had been lying against the fence. His tail began to wag again—he knew this game! He began to pull hard against the leash. Jack squeaked and sprang onto his scooter as Bear raced down the path, Jack and the scooter bumping and rattling behind him. They bounced and clattered toward the park gates, with Jack giggling and Bear panting happily. Playing with Jack was his favorite thing to do.

Chapter Two
Meeting Bear

Jade kicked the tennis ball toward the fence, catching it with the side of her foot on the rebound. She kept on tapping and catching the ball until at last it bounced off into a flower bed and she had to crawl through the bushes to find it. It was one of Honey's old toy balls, Jade realized, as she picked it up. She used to throw it for Honey to fetch all the time.

Jade wandered back up the length of the yard with the ball in her hand. What would it be like to have another dog? Honey would have been out here with her, racing up and down, desperate to play. Even though she'd slowed down a lot in her last year, she still loved to run. Jade had even built her an agility course out of old flowerpots and garden sticks—she'd been very good at weaving in between them. It would be a lot of fun to teach a puppy to do things like that.... Jade smiled to herself, imagining that beautiful puppy from the park trying to fit between the sticks. From the look of it, the puppy was the perfect size now, but it wouldn't be long before it was too big.

She left the ball on the patio bench and hurried inside, remembering that she'd wanted to find out what kind of dog it was. She started off looking at the dog-breed poster on her bedroom wall, but she'd been right, it definitely wasn't on there. It was a little similar to the sheepdogs, but the coloring wasn't quite the same, and Jade was sure it was bigger all over. She grabbed her book of dog breeds off the shelf instead and started to flip through. She had a feeling that maybe the puppy was some kind of shepherd dog, so she started off in the Working Dogs section, laughing at the photo of a massive black Newfoundland. It really did look like a teddy bear.

Then she turned a couple of pages, and her face lit up in a smile. "Yes! That's you!" The dog in the book was fully grown, not a puppy like the one she'd seen, but the markings were almost identical. "A Bernese mountain dog...," Jade muttered. She'd never even heard of them before. One of the smaller photos showed two Bernese mountain dogs pulling a little cart with two toddlers sitting in it. It made it clear just how

enormous the dogs were. "These giants are gentle but determined," Jade read aloud to herself, leaning back against her bedroom wall and smiling. She was trying to imagine that adorable, chunky puppy all grown up. It was going to be so handsome.

The next day, Jade kept a hopeful eye out as she and her mom headed home from school through the park, looking for the Bernese mountain dog. She gave a delighted squeak as they got close enough to see the playground. Her mom glanced at her in surprise. "What is it? Have you seen one of your friends?"

"No, it's that puppy! Oh, I forgot, you didn't see it yesterday—it was Dad." Jade's mom and dad took turns picking her up from school—it depended on who was working where. Luckily, they both got to work from home some of the time. "It's a Bernese mountain dog, I think. I looked it up last night. It's so cute."

Jade's mom peered at the dog across the park. "It looks big."

"If it is a Bernese, it's going to be enormous. They can pull carts!" Jade looked sideways at her mom. "I sort of accidentally petted it…. I didn't mean to! I wasn't looking and it licked me, and I patted its ears…."

Her mom rolled her eyes. "Why am I not surprised?"

Jade giggled. "But I'd really like to see who it belongs to, so I could ask if I could pet it. And maybe find out what its name is."

"Well, you're in luck." Her mom nodded toward the puppy. "I think that must be its owner, with the stroller."

"Oh, yay! Hurry up, Mom." Jade grabbed her mom's arm and started to tow her across the park. There was a little boy standing close to the puppy now, too. He was wearing the same school uniform as Jade. "Oh, he goes to Gardner Elementary, too. I don't think I've ever talked to him, though. He looks like he's in kindergarten or first grade, maybe."

As they came closer to the little

group around the puppy, Jade slowed down a bit, feeling shy. The lady with the stroller was strapping in a little girl, and she looked up curiously as Jade came over to her.

"Um, hi!" Jade felt her cheeks turn pink. "I just wanted to ask about your dog.... Is it a Bernese mountain dog?"

The puppy's owner smiled at her. "Yes! Most people don't know what he is."

"His name is Bear!" the little boy told Jade proudly. "He's from Switzerland."

"Sort of," his mom agreed. "Bear didn't actually come all the way from Switzerland, did he, Jack? But Bernese mountain dogs are from Switzerland."

"I saw him here yesterday, and I went and looked it up," Jade admitted. "I hadn't heard of Bernese mountain dogs before. He's beautiful."

"You can pet him, if you like," the puppy's owner told her. "He can be a little nervous sometimes, though, so be careful. He does jump up."

Jade nodded, moving a little closer to Bear, but not looking him straight in the eyes. It was the way Mom had explained it was best to get to know a dog—to let the dog come to her, instead of marching right up and expecting the dog not to mind being patted or hugged.

The big puppy sniffed at her eagerly, his heavy tail waving, and then nudged his cold nose into her hand. Jade crouched down and ran her hand gently along his back.

"You're very good with him," his owner commented, smiling at her.

"He's beautiful!" Jade told her. "Oh!" She looked on a little worriedly as Jack bounced up behind Bear and tried to pet him, too. The puppy backed away as the little boy grabbed at his collar, his paws skittering on the cement.

"Careful now, Jack." His mom leaned over, whispering gently to the dog. "It's okay, Bear. Good boy."

27

Jack looked at Bear and Jade anxiously. Jade could see Jack didn't really understand what he'd done wrong—he had just wanted to hug his big teddy-bear dog. He probably didn't realize that he was making Bear feel scared. She smiled at him. "You're so lucky to have him," she said. "He's so big and so fluffy!"

"Yes!" Jack agreed, cheering up. "He pulls me along on my scooter. He's really strong."

"We need to be getting home now," Jack's mom said. "Say good-bye, Jack." She smiled at Jade and her mom. "Maybe we'll see you in the park tomorrow. It's nice for Jack to talk to one of the older children from school. We just moved here, and he's having to get used to a new class. It's great having this park so close to the school, though."

Jade nodded—so that was why she hadn't seen Bear around before. She knew almost all the dogs in the park to say hello to, since they walked through it every day on the way home from school.

"'Bye! See you tomorrow!" She watched Bear and Jack and his mom heading off down the path, feeling a little envious.

"Isn't he beautiful?" she said to her mom as they set off for the park gate.

"He really is," her mom agreed. "I'm not sure I'd be able to cope with two small children and a huge dog, though. Jack's mom must be even more of a dog fan than you."

Jade grinned at her. "Not possible."

Over the next couple of weeks, Jade saw Bear and his family almost every day after school, and sometimes on the way to school, too—Jack's mom, Lauren, brought him with her when she dropped Jack off. Jade's mom and Lauren chatted with each other. Jade's mom said she thought Lauren was lonely—the family had moved because Jack's dad had gotten a new job, and she didn't know that many people in the area yet. It was nice for Jack, too— Jade always said hello to him at recess. She even heard some of the other boys in his class asking Jack if she was his sister. It made him look cool, knowing one of the older children.

"You can't wait to get to the park and look for that dog, can you," Jade's dad said, laughing at her as she hurried along the sidewalk one afternoon. He heaved a dramatic sigh. "I wish you were that excited about seeing me…."

"Oh, Dad…," Jade raced back and hugged him. "I do like seeing you— but—"

"I'm not a dog, I know."

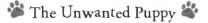

"There they are!" Jade waved to Jack, who was on the path up ahead. The kindergarten class came out 10 minutes before the rest of the school, so Jack was usually at the park before they got there. Jack didn't wave back, though—he seemed to be arguing with his mom, and Jade wasn't sure he'd noticed them coming up behind.

"I want to go on the slide!" He glared angrily at his mom.

Jade hung back—she wanted to say hello to Bear, who was looking miserable, but she didn't want to make anything worse.

"I know you do," his mom said patiently. "But Bear hasn't had a good walk today! I was late picking up Tina from the babysitter this morning, so Bear missed his walk. We don't have time for both, Jack, and it's not fair to Bear to make him sit outside at the playground right now...."

"It's not fair to *me*!" Jack wailed. "I want to go on the slide!" Then he noticed Jade and her dad, dawdling along the path. "She can take Bear for a walk."

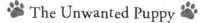

"Oh...." Jack's mom glanced around and smiled at Jade, and then at her dad, looking a little embarrassed. "I'm sorry, Jack, but no. That's silly."

"I could take him for a run, if that would help," Jade put in eagerly. "I mean, if that's okay, Dad?"

Her dad nodded. "We've got time." He shrugged his shoulders at Lauren, grinning. "Jade used to get really upset if I wouldn't let her go on the swings.... I know how you feel."

Lauren smiled, looking relieved. "Oh, if you really wouldn't mind, that would be such a help. We're having trouble fitting proper walks in right now. Jack's dad always used to walk Bear at lunchtime, but he can't do that with his new job. Bear knows you, so I'm sure he'd love it. Just be careful, Jade, because he *is* very strong. And don't let him off the leash, okay? He's not good at coming back. We need to do some more obedience classes, but I haven't found a session we can get to yet."

Jade nodded. "I'll make sure I'm holding him tightly. And Dad will be there, too." She beamed at her dad as Jack's mom put the leash into her hand, and Bear pulled eagerly, his tail suddenly speeding up. The park was huge—she and Mom and Dad used to bring Honey there almost every day.

"Should we run?" she whispered to Bear. "Should we? Would you like that?"

Bear's tail wagged even faster, and

he gave a tiny woof. Jade laughed and raced off across the grass with the puppy bounding beside her, his ears flapping and his paws thumping the grass.

It was the best feeling ever.

Chapter Three
Bear in Trouble!

Bear paced up and down the kitchen, whining over and over. He was worried and lonely. Everyone was out, and he wasn't used to it. Usually either Lauren or her husband, Ben, was home, and he felt safe. Even if Lauren or Ben weren't paying attention to him, he knew that they were there. But over the last few days, they had been going out and

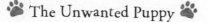

leaving him behind for what seemed like forever. It made him miserable. He didn't understand what was going on, and he wanted his people back.

He had watched Lauren and Jack and baby Tina leaving this morning, and he realized that it was going to happen again. What if they never came back? He had started to whine, but Lauren hadn't understood that he was worried, and Jack had just told him to shush.

Bear was tired, and his basket was right there, nice and warm by the radiator, but he couldn't seem to stop pacing. Maybe he'd never see them again! He whined louder and then slumped down suddenly, lifting his nose to the ceiling in a long howl, fear and loneliness taking over for a moment. He lay on the kitchen floor, howling and howling, until there was a loud thumping against the wall and a muffled shouting. Bear didn't understand that it was the man next door, annoyed by the noise, but he could tell that the shouting was angry, and it frightened him even more.

Anxiously, he slunk into the living room, away from the kitchen and the scary shouting. He tucked himself away behind the end of the couch—it was a tight fit for such a big puppy, but he felt safer in the small space.

He was still upset, though.

Bear listened, hunched and tense in the tiny space, wondering if the angry noises were still going on. The panicked feeling inside him was building again, and he pawed anxiously at the side of the couch, scratching harder and harder with his claws. Somehow, the clawing seemed to help him feel a little calmer, and he kept doing it, shredding the fabric with his claws until it hung down from the couch in tattered ribbons. There was yellow foamy stuff behind the fabric and that pulled out, too, if he bit at it. Bear scratched and chewed and gnawed, and some of the miserable feeling inside him went away.

Bear heard the footsteps coming to the door, and he jumped up, full of relief and excitement. They were back! They hadn't abandoned him! He dashed to the door and leaped at it, his paws slipping and sliding on the smooth wood. He could hear Lauren laughing on the other side of the door.

"Hello! Hello, Bear! Yes, we're back. Did you miss us? I know, it's not fair, is it? I didn't have time to come and get you before I went to get Jack. Are you hungry?" She nudged Bear gently out of the way so she could get the stroller over the front step. "No running out. Good boy. Hey, don't jump up...." Lauren pushed Tina inside and turned to shut the door.

Bear knew he wasn't supposed to jump up at the stroller, but he was so desperate to see them all—to love them, to show his family how much he had missed them.

"No, down," Lauren said firmly, and Bear backed off from the stroller and turned to greet Jack instead. But the little boy stumbled away from Bear's scratchy paws as the puppy tried to jump up and lick his face.

"Mommy! He's hurting me!" The frightened tone in Jack's voice made Bear's ears flatten, and he backed away. Had he done something wrong? He just wanted to be with them....

"Mommy, look!" Jack was standing in the living-room doorway, staring at the couch and the floor. Lauren lifted Tina out of the stroller and followed him in.

"What's the matter? Oh, *no*...."

"Was it Bear?" Jack asked, and hearing his name, Bear looked at them worriedly. Their voices were angry.

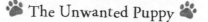
"It must have been. It's ruined. The new couch! Oh, you bad dog!"

Bear retreated down the tiny hallway, his head hanging and his bottom in a crouch. What had he done? He'd been so desperate to see them, and now Lauren was angry. He just didn't understand.

"Hi, Jade!"

Jade looked around from where she was chatting with her friend Lucy and waved at Jack, smiling. A group of kindergarten children were kicking a ball around the playground.

"Hi! Are you playing soccer with the others?"

"Yes—I just came to tell you about yesterday. Guess what Bear did!"

"I don't know…. Um…. Did he pull you to school on your scooter?"

"No! He chewed up our couch! He really wrecked it. Mom was so angry. We came in from school, and there were pieces of it all over the floor. She had to put a blanket over the end of it so we could watch TV; otherwise, we'd have been sitting *in* the couch!"

"Oh, no. Why did he chew it up?"

Jack shrugged. "Don't know. Mom said maybe he didn't like being left on his own when she had to go to work and Dad did, too."

Jade nodded. Some dogs really hated being on their own. Honey hadn't liked it much, either, but luckily, her mom

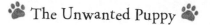

and dad had managed to work their shifts around taking care of Jade and being home enough of the time that Honey didn't get too upset. And sometimes her grandma had popped in to see Honey if they were going to be away for more than a couple of hours.

"Mom shut him in the kitchen today—there's not much he can chew in there, she said."

That doesn't sound like much of a fun day for Bear, Jade thought. *Locked up in the kitchen.* She wondered if Lauren would bring him to school to pick up Jack that afternoon. She'd missed seeing him the day before because she had soccer practice after school, but it sounded like Lauren hadn't brought Bear on the school run anyway.

"I've got to go, it's my turn in goal! See you later, Jade!" Jack suddenly raced away, and Jade waved after him. She watched Jack running around with his friends and bit her lip, feeling worried. Jack seemed to be really settling in, but what if Bear was getting himself into more trouble, stuck at home on his own?

Chapter Four
A Great Idea

When Jade came out of school, she spotted her mom waiting for her in the playground.

"See you tomorrow!" Jade called, waving good-bye to Lucy.

"Did you have a good day?" her mom asked, giving her a hug.

"Mm-hmm." Jade nodded. "Oh, Mom, look! Bear's here!"

Her mom looked around. "What, in school? I thought dogs weren't allowed in the playground."

"No, over there by the gate." Jade pointed to the puppy, whose leash was tied to the railing. He was watching the children streaming out of the gate and wagging his tail at them hopefully. "He doesn't seem worried, does he?"

Her mom looked confused. "Why would he be worried?"

"I was talking to Jack at lunchtime, and he said that Bear had chewed up

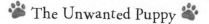

the couch yesterday when he was on his own. Jack said he really wrecked it. But he doesn't look as though he minds being left alone right now."

Her mom sighed. "Ugh, I remember Honey doing things like that. Once she scratched all around the carpet by the front door!"

"Did she?" Jade blinked. She didn't remember that.

"Yes, but you were very young. It was before we figured out that we needed to get Grandma or Anna next door to pop in and see her if we were out for a long time. And I got her one of those toys that you can put treats in, which helped a little."

Jade nodded. "That's clever—did it stop her from worrying?"

"I think so. She was distracted by the toy. We put peanut butter in it sometimes, and she loved that."

Lauren and Jack caught up with Jade and her mom as they were threading their way down the path out of school, and Jade's mom smiled. "Hello! You're out later than usual."

Lauren nodded. "Jack couldn't find his lunchbox. It took us a while to track it down."

"Are you going to the park?" Jade asked hopefully as Lauren undid Bear's leash. Bear nudged his nose affectionately into Jade's hand, and she smiled to herself at the chilly feel of it.

Lauren laughed. "Yes. We need to work off some of Bear's energy. He's really not liking being at home without

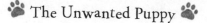

us now that I'm working."

"Jack told me about the couch," Jade said, making a face.

"Our old dog, Honey, used to chew things when she was on her own," Jade's mom said with a sigh. "I remember feeling as though everything had to be up on a shelf!"

"The couch has a big hole in it!" Jack told Jade's mom. "Bear was so naughty."

Jade thought Lauren looked suddenly tired, and she felt guilty for reminding her about it. "I'm not sure what we're going to do," she said, sighing. "We love Bear, but he's a handful to take care of, and he's growing so much! We knew how big he was going to get—we'd seen his mom. But I don't think we really understood…. He's almost the same size as Jack already."

"But he's friendly, isn't he?" Jade asked, looking at Bear ambling along beside Jack. He really did look like a teddy bear. She couldn't imagine him being fierce.

"Absolutely! Bernese mountain dogs are really good with children; that's why we wanted to get one. It's just that Bear can easily knock Jack or Tina over when he's excited. I hadn't realized how strong he was going to be. And he really does need a good long walk every day. It wasn't much of a problem before—Jack's dad used to take him out. But since he's changed jobs, and I'm back at work, too…." She sighed. "I think yesterday was just too much for him. He must have been really lonely. Luckily I didn't have to work so many hours today."

"Do you have any family locally who could pop in and check on him while you're out?" Jade's mom asked.

"No. All our relatives live close to our old house. We weren't planning to move, but then Ben's new job came up. We love our new house, and the new school—it has all worked out— except it hasn't worked out that well for Bear."

"Jade, will you push me on the swings?" Jack asked hopefully, pulling her hand as they walked along the path to the little playground in the park.

"'Course." Jade grinned at him. She wanted to pet Bear, and maybe be allowed to take him for a run again, but she liked playing with Jack, too. It was like having a little brother. She followed him toward the fenced-off playground, and Jack gave the gate a push and it swung open. Jade wondered if she should close the bolt that was supposed to stop the little ones from running out, but she could see two little girls and their dad coming, so she didn't. People were always leaving the gate open.

She pushed Jack on the swings for a while, and then he jumped off and ran over to the jungle gym, clambering

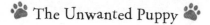

up the sloping climbing wall to get to the slide. Jade glanced over—her mom and Jack's mom were chatting by the playground gate, and it didn't look like Mom was in a hurry to go. She stood there half watching Jack and half admiring Bear. He was watching them, too, looking as though he wished he could be with them.

"I'm good at climbing, aren't I?" Jack said to her hopefully, and Jade turned back to smile at him.

"Really good! You got up there so fast." Jade glanced over as she heard the gate clang again and gasped. Bear was dashing toward them, his leash bouncing on the ground. He must have pulled it out of Jack's mom's hand.

Jade glanced at her mom and Jack's mom and saw that they were still by the gate, looking horrified. Jack's mom was staring at her hand, as though she wasn't quite sure what had happened. Then she hurried toward the playground, calling, "Bear! No! Come back!"

"What's that dog doing in here?" one of the moms over by the seesaw said angrily. "Who does it belong to? No, Cindy, don't go near it!"

"He's not fierce—" Jade started to say as Bear came up to her, wagging his tail happily. Jade picked up his leash and gently rubbed his ears. Jack stood at the top of the jungle gym and glared at the dog. "You're not supposed to be in here, Bear! Bad dog!"

Bear looked up at Jade worriedly,

as though he thought she might scold him, too. The mom who'd been standing by the seesaw was marching toward them, and Jade could see that Bear was scared of her. His ears flattened, and he started to lick at his nose anxiously. "It's okay," she whispered.

"That dog shouldn't be in here!" the mom snapped at Jade, but luckily Jack's mom came over just in time.

"I'm really sorry—his leash slipped out of my hand. Come on, Bear." She took the leash from Jade with a whispered, "Thank you!" and hurried out, ignoring the mom behind her muttering about people who didn't train their dogs properly.

Jack slid down the slide and put his hand in Jade's. "Is she upset with us?" he asked, nodding at the other mom.

"Only a little. Should we go and find your mom?"

"I'm so sorry, Jade. I hope that lady didn't upset you," Jack's mom said worriedly, winding Bear's leash tightly around her hand. "Bear just pulled away from me—I think he wanted to play with you and Jack."

"It was an accident." Jade's mom patted Lauren on the arm. "Don't worry about it."

"He didn't do anything really bad." Jade smiled at Jack's mom. "It's fine."

She glanced between her mom and Jack's mom. "I could take him for another run, like I did the other day, if you want. If it's okay with you, Mom?"

Her mom smiled at her. "I don't mind. Actually, Lauren, I was going to say, if you're ever stuck, I know Jade would love to walk him. She hasn't stopped talking about how handsome Bear is since she met him. We'd very happily exercise him for you after school if it would help. We could do most days, I think. Jade has soccer practice after school on Wednesdays, but that's all. We really miss having a dog around."

"Yes!" Jade nodded. "It would be like we were borrowing him." She crouched down to run her hand along Bear's back, and he nudged her chin lovingly.

"You really wouldn't mind?" Lauren asked. "It would be great for him to have more exercise. I think it would help a lot with him being lonely at home if he was tired out!" She looked worriedly at Jade's mom. "I don't want us to be a bother, though. It's a lot to ask. I feel like we should be able to take care of him by ourselves."

"It would be great for us, honestly," Jade's mom promised, and Jade smiled at Bear, who was leaning against her heavily as she scratched his back.

"How could anyone ever think you were a bother?" she whispered in his ear.

Bear pulled a little against his leash, looking up at Jade hopefully. He felt bouncy, full of energy, as if he could just run and run. Was Jade going to let him

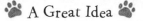

race across the park with her, the way they had before? She had dashed back and forth, laughing and panting and chasing after him, and she'd never once had to stop and tie him up to a fence, or walk slowly to match the stroller. It had just been fun.

"Should we go for a run?" Jade asked him, crouching down to give his ears a rub.

Bear barked. He knew that word. He skittered backward, telling Jade to come on, and Jade laughed at him.

Chapter Five
The Escape

"Morning, sweetie." Jade's dad pushed the cereal box across the table toward her. Then he laughed. "I had to wake you up three times this morning, and you still don't look awake."

"Ughhh." Jade sighed and poured herself some cornflakes. "I can't believe it's only Friday. It has to be the weekend."

Her dad shook his head sadly. "Nope. Definitely Friday, sorry. Eat up fast, Jade, because you have breakfast club today. You don't want to be late for your second breakfast!"

Jade made a face as she poured on some milk.

"What? Don't you like breakfast club? I thought it was okay. Lucy goes, too, doesn't she?"

"Mm-hmm. It's just if I go to school early, I don't get to watch for Jack and Lauren bringing Bear with them." She smiled at her dad. "He keeps an eye out for me, you know? He looks all around the school playground and when he sees me, his tail speeds up like a ... like a ceiling fan."

Her dad nodded. "Ah.... Sorry, Jade. You really like that dog, don't you?" he added, stirring his cereal thoughtfully.

"He's the best." Jade looked across at her dad and realized that she was stirring her bowl just like he was. "But I'm worried about him, Dad...."

"Why?"

Jade sighed, trying to figure out how to say it. "Jack really loves Bear, and so does his mom, but he gets into a lot of trouble. He chewed their couch to pieces, and Jack's always telling me about how he knocked something over, or chewed something else. Jack's mom is so busy taking care of Tina and working and everything. And his dad works really long hours, so he's not home a lot." She hesitated. "It's like Bear's always the thing that comes last."

Her dad frowned. "I don't know if that's fair, Jade. They take him for walks—we see them in the park with him almost every day."

"Yes, but that's not a proper walk! He just gets to come along on the way to school! He needs *long* walks. He's such a big dog—and he's still only a puppy. He'll need more when he's bigger."

Her dad nodded slowly. "You really

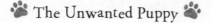

are worried about this, aren't you?"

"Yes." Jade heaved a huge sigh. "But we can't actually do anything about it. I mean, except help out by taking him for walks when we can. Mom told Jack's mom yesterday that I could take him for a run if we see them in the park after school."

"Mmmm...." Her dad swallowed a mouthful of tea. "Those Bernese mountain dogs do need a lot of exercise. Not just walks, either. Their brains need exercise. Obedience classes, or agility."

"How do you know?" Jade asked, very surprised. She was pretty sure her dad hadn't known what a Bernese was until she'd told him.

Her dad looked a little embarrassed. "Ummm. I might have looked them up.

A couple of websites…. Stop laughing at me! He's such a nice dog, I just wondered about them, that's all."

Jade stared at her dad, feeling as though pieces in her brain were clicking into place. "You mean, maybe one day we could get one? You're thinking about it?"

"Maybe. And I haven't even mentioned it to your mom, Jade, so you'd better not."

Jade grinned at him.

"Finish your cereal!"

Bear peered into the hallway. He could hear people passing on the street outside—children's voices, high and squeaky, like Jack. He was sure that Lauren and Jack and Tina would be coming home soon. It felt like way past time for a walk.

Since the day Bear had chewed the couch to shreds, when he was home alone, he had to stay in the kitchen. Lauren and Ben had bought him a special toy to keep him busy while they were gone, and he loved it. It wobbled around, bouncing over the floor as he nudged it with his nose or smacked it with a paw. He had to hit it just right to get the food out. But it was empty now, and it had been for hours, it felt like. Restlessly, Bear paced around the table again, and then again.

Then he stopped, his ears twitching eagerly. Was that voices? Footsteps outside the front door? It was hard to tell through two shut doors, but he was almost sure…. Bear started to bark frantically, jumping and scratching at the kitchen door. It was already scarred with long scratches, the wood shredding under his claws. He could hear the front door opening now and Lauren heaving in the stroller. Jack was laughing. Oh, how he wanted to get out of there!

"Listen to that dog! Go and let him out, Jack. I wish I'd been able to pick him up before I came to get you, but I couldn't get out of work in time."

Bear jumped and barked even louder, desperate to see his family. As Jack opened the kitchen door Bear flung himself forward, wanting to lick them all over—to show them how much he'd missed them.

He hurled himself through the door, not realizing that Jack was standing just behind it. Bear went straight into him, his front paws right on the little boy's chest, and Jack flew backward, landing on the hallway floor with a thud.

"Jack!"

Jack was silent for a moment, until he caught his breath, and then he howled.

Bear stared at him, horrified by the noise. He wasn't entirely sure what had happened—was Jack playing? They did roll on the floor together sometimes. He leaned over and nudged Jack's cheek with his nose.

"Bad dog! Get away!" Lauren scolded, and Bear flinched. He crept along the wall to hide in the corner by the front door where the boots were. It had all been so quick. He'd only wanted to say hello—it had been such a long day shut in the kitchen all by himself....

Bear watched as Lauren picked Jack up, fussing over him and smoothing his hair anxiously. Jack was still crying, and now Tina was wailing, too. Bear pressed further into the corner, trying to make himself small enough so that no one would see him and shout.

Bear finished his bowl of food and looked over at Lauren, wondering when he was going for a walk. She'd let him into the yard to go to the bathroom, but that was all. He hadn't been out since Ben had taken him for a quick sprint along the road and back that morning before he left for work. Bear slumped down by the back door sadly, thinking of Jade racing him across the park and laughing. He was bored—and he felt lonely, even though his people were right here. Jack was still angry with him, he could tell. He kept glaring whenever

Bear looked at him.

When Ben got back, Bear bounced up to him hopefully, but all he got was a quick ear scratch, and then Jack grabbed his dad's hand and climbed up his legs for a hug, telling him all about his accident.

"I banged my head on the floor! I really did. It went thump. Mommy shouted at Bear!"

"Oh, no, love, what happened?" Ben looked over at Lauren anxiously.

"It wasn't really Bear's fault. I think he jumped up just at the wrong time. He was so excited to see us—you know he hates being shut in on his own while we're all out." Lauren sighed. "He just plowed Jack over. He's getting so strong...."

Jack's dad hugged him tighter and made sympathetic noises about the lump on his head, and then Jack wriggled away and went back to playing with his cars.

"Do you think he's okay? He doesn't look as if it's hurting that much," Ben said, shrugging off his jacket and sitting down at the table.

"I think he's fine—this time. I was so worried, though." Lauren shook her head. "I just don't know what we're going to do, Ben…."

Ben made a face. "I know. We weren't expecting the new job and the move to happen, that's all. When we first got Bear, we had plenty of time to take care of him. But now—we're not doing a very good job, are we, boy?"

Bear hurried over to him, resting his muzzle lovingly on Ben's leg. He closed his eyes blissfully as Ben pulled gently on his ears. Yes! At last someone was fussing over him, like he wanted.

Then there was a sudden wail from the hallway, and a furious shout from Jack. "Tina took my car!"

Ben jumped up to go and sort out the argument, gently pushing Bear away, and that was that. Everyone seemed to be busy, racing around and hardly noticing him at all.

Bear gave up and took his chew toy over to the nest he'd made among the boots. There was a little draft coming in under the front door—a fresh scent of outdoors and the cut-grass smell of the park.

I could go by myself, Bear thought sadly, pressing his nose against the crack. He knew the way. He might even find Jade. His tail thumped on the carpet at the thought of her. Yes! He would go to the park and find Jade—she was always there when he was. Why shouldn't he?

It was just then that he heard footsteps hurrying up to the door, and the doorbell rang. Bear jumped back in surprise at the shrill noise, his tail swishing uncertainly. He watched as Jack came racing down the hall shouting,

"Nana! Nana!" and reached up to open the front door.

There was someone on the doorstep, but Bear hardly saw them. He only saw the path and the sidewalk and the swinging gate in between.

The sidewalk led to the park and to Jade—someone who wanted him. He raced out the door before anyone could stop him.

Chapter Six
Looking for Jade

Jade sat on her bed, with her mom's laptop balanced on the pillow. All day at school she'd been thinking about her conversation with her dad—the amazing idea that maybe they could have a Bernese mountain dog of their own!

Jade had been hoping to meet up with Bear and Jack and Jack's mom in the park after school and take Bear for a walk—she'd thought maybe she'd also get the chance to ask Jack's mom about a fun agility class or something like that for Bear. It might help to wear him out and keep his brain busy. She'd been sort of looking forward to asking about it, and sort of not. She didn't want Jack's mom to think she was sticking her nose in....

Jade sighed. She hadn't realized until today just how much she looked forward to seeing Bear—she'd been so disappointed to miss him. Meeting up with him in the park was one of the highlights of her day. Jade was almost sure that her mom and dad felt the same. She'd noticed that she and Mom both sped up as they went in the park

gates on the way home from school.
They'd hurry along the paths, scanning
the park to see where Bear was. Dad
was just the same, always
looking hopefully for the
big puppy on their
walk to school.

Today
they hadn't
seen him
at all—Jade
had met Jack
and his mom
and Tina
hurrying through the
playground, and Jack's mom had
explained that she hadn't had time to
go home and get Bear that afternoon.
She'd even been a little late picking

Jack up, she said. Jade felt as though she'd missed out on something special. She sighed again and peered thoughtfully at the list of websites on the screen. There seemed to be tons of links to pages about Bernese mountain dogs—some were the websites for Bernese rescues and some were clubs for owners. She chose one of the club pages and clicked on *Things to Know*. If Dad was really serious about them getting a Bernese one day, she wanted to be prepared.

Jade found herself nodding thoughtfully as she read the page. A lot of the information seemed to tie in with what she'd noticed about Bear. She'd seen him start to look worried and jumpy when Tina was crying,

and it said on the page that some Bernese could be sound-sensitive—that high-pitched noises almost hurt their ears.

Jade nibbled her lip worriedly. Jack's mom had said Tina was teething and crying a lot. That definitely wasn't going to help Bear settle down. There were common-sense things the website said to think about, too—a big dog was more likely to accidentally hurt a small child. Bear was big, but he was still a puppy, so he was clumsy and not really in control of his paws....

Jade went on reading, giggling to herself at some of the funny parts. Apparently most Bernese didn't really like playing fetch, because they just didn't see the point. The owner would throw a ball, and the dog would fetch it the first couple of times and then give up, because honestly, *why?* She could easily imagine Bear dropping a ball at her feet and glaring at her, his beautiful orange eyebrows twitching. *Now, look. You keep dropping it, and I keep bringing it back to you. Don't do it again! Hey! I said don't do that....* It would be so funny.

Jade looked up from the laptop, her eyes widening. Then she turned herself around on the bed, sinking her chin into her hands. She'd just realized something—something awful.

Dad was all excited about getting a puppy, but she didn't want just any Bernese mountain dog.

She wanted Bear.

Bear raced down the sidewalk, ignoring the shouts behind him. It was so good not to be cooped up in the house! His paws pounded on the cement, and his ears were flapping as he bounded along. It was a chilly evening and a little bit drizzly, but he didn't mind. The dampness felt good on his fur.

He paused for a moment at the end of the road, sniffing thoughtfully. Ben usually took him out for a short walk just before bed, so he was used to the dark. Yes, the park was this way. He trotted on, eager to go racing over the grass and find Jade. As he saw the park gates ahead he sped up, and his tail started to wag with excitement. He darted in, loving the scents of cut grass and tree blossoms and other dogs. He bounced onto the wide stretch of grass, enjoying the feel of the soft ground and cool grass under his paws.

For a couple of minutes he just ran, feeling the stretch in his legs as he snapped at imaginary butterflies and chased his own tail around and around. Then he slumped down into a happy, panting heap and started to wonder where Jade was.

He had expected to find her—or rather, he'd expected her to find *him*. She always did. He looked around eagerly, hoping to see her hurrying down the path toward him, excited and waving. But there seemed to be no one in the park at all. It was eerily quiet.

Bear sat up and gazed around worriedly. He hadn't thought about what he might do if he couldn't find Jade. He had just expected that she would be there. She always was....

Except maybe this time she wasn't.... His ears twitched at the strange sounds of the birds rustling in the trees and he stood up, pacing around in a tiny circle. Jade was in the park when he was there with Jack, Bear realized. Now it was the wrong time—it was dark, closer to the time he went out for a last walk before bed.

Jade wasn't here. He was all alone.

Tucked away under the little climbing wall that led up to the playground slide, Bear gazed out at the damp morning, wondering if he should try to find his way back home. He was sure he could do it—he'd done this walk so many times. But something was stopping him. He kept remembering Jack howling when he'd knocked him over by accident, and then Lauren's sharp voice. They had both sounded so angry and upset.

Somehow his home wasn't a place

he felt happy in anymore, and Bear didn't really understand how that had happened.

A few times during the night the cold had woken him, and Bear had wanted to go home. But the padding of strange paws past his hiding place had made him tuck his tail between his legs and wriggle farther under the leaves in the corner, and he wished he'd never run away. He knew home. He was safe there, at least, and warm. A couple of times he'd gotten as far as the gate of the little playground before he remembered how angry everyone was and how he hated being shut in the kitchen on his own. Each time, he'd turned back from the gate and gone to curl up by himself again.

Now Bear's tail thumped against the dry leaves as he heard voices in the distance. Jade! She'd come to find him at last! He wriggled out of his hiding place just as a dad with two little girls pushed open the gate. Bear's tail drooped again as one of the little girls raced toward the climbing wall and then stopped.

"A dog!" she squeaked. Bear came out from under the sloping wall, his tail beating nervously from side to side.

"Hey, Olivia, come here!" the little girl's father said sharply. "Don't touch the dog. We don't know if it's friendly. It must be a stray—there's no one else here."

The little girl ran back toward her father, and he shooed her and her sister out of the way. Then he came closer to Bear, crouching low and flapping his hands. "Come on. Out!"

Bear tucked his tail down, crouching. He'd done something wrong again, he could tell. These people were upset with him, too. He scuttled forward, trying to avoid the angry-sounding man, and darted out of the gate.

Now that he was up and walking, Bear realized how hungry he was. Maybe he should just go home after all. But the path back to the gate led past the playground again. He didn't want to go that way and be shouted at. So he kept going, wandering along the path that led to the other side of the big park and another gate. He didn't usually come this way with Lauren and Jack and he stood uncertainly in the opening, wondering where to go and what to do.

He felt more alone than ever.

Chapter Seven
Found!

"But I thought *all* dogs liked playing fetch! You mean they don't even chase sticks?" Jade thought her dad sounded shocked. She grinned at him, shrugging. It was so exciting talking to him about Bernese dogs like this. It made it seem all the more possible that they might get another dog of their own soon. *Even if it's not*

Bear ... a little voice said in the back of her mind. Jade squashed it down again. Bear belonged to another family. He was Jack's dog. She was going to have her *own* dog.

"That's what this website said. I guess chasing sticks might be different.... I don't know. It just said they think fetching is boring. I can see why, can't you?"

"Mm-hmm. It really does sound as though they're very intelligent." Jade's dad glanced down at his watch. "We'd better walk a little faster if we're going to get to this dance class on time, Jade. It's almost 10!"

Jade wasn't listening. "Dad, look!" She grabbed his arm. "Look! Isn't that Bear?"

"What? Oh, are they out for a walk?" Her dad looked up and down the street, obviously expecting to see Lauren or Ben.

"No, look! There behind that parked car. *It is!*"

Jade stuffed her dance bag into Dad's arms and raced up the road. She was almost sure that the black and tan and white dog peering around the car was Bear, but he was all by himself. Lauren never let him off the leash, because he wasn't good about coming back.

"Did you pull your leash out of her

hand?" Jade asked gently, stopping a little ways from Bear and the car. He looked nervous, and she didn't want to scare him and make him run into the road. But he darted toward her, licking her hands and whining delightedly. "Hello! Oh, you're such a handsome dog! But where's your family, Bear? Where's Jack?"

"Hello, boy," her dad panted. "So it is you...." He crouched down to pet Bear, too. "Can you see Lauren or Ben, Jade? Bear shouldn't be out on the sidewalk like this."

"I know," said Jade. "I thought he must have pulled his leash out of someone's hand, but he doesn't even have his leash on. Just his collar. And they don't let him off the leash...."

"Ohhh…. Have you run away?" Dad muttered to Bear, rubbing his ears. "Maybe he slipped out of their yard."

"What are we going to do?" Jade asked. "We should take him home, but I only know they live on the other side of the park. I think they go to the gate at the bottom of the hill."

"Hmmm." Dad looked thoughtful. "We could walk down that way; we might meet them coming to look for him. But then we're not even sure if they know he's gone…. Oh! Dance class!" He looked at his watch again and made a face. "Jade, it's starting right now!"

"But taking Bear home is way more important," Jade said indignantly. "We can text Miss Julia. She won't mind, Dad, honestly."

"Well, I guess you're right. We can't just leave him here. Does he have a tag on that collar?"

"Yes, and there's a phone number. We can call them."

Dad sighed. "Except that I don't my phone with me. We'll have to take him home and do it." He unzipped Jade's dance bag. "Do you think we could tie your ballet tights through his collar? I don't want to risk him running out into the road."

Jade laughed. "Yes, but we'd better not tell Mom. She said those tights were really expensive."

Carefully, she looped the tights through Bear's collar and turned to lead him gently back toward their house. "Come on, Bear…." She wasn't sure if he'd want to follow her—after all, he didn't know her that well, and he wasn't used to going in this direction. But he padded along beside her quite happily, every now and then looking up at her as if to check that she was still there.

"He's walking very well," Dad said. "Not pulling at all. I was a little worried he'd be too strong for you, but he's being very calm."

"He's beautiful," Jade said with a tiny sigh. She wished it was a longer walk home. As soon as they called the cell phone number on his collar, Lauren or Ben would come and pick up Bear, and it was so wonderful pretending that he was hers and they were just out for a weekend stroll.

She led Bear into their driveway, and Dad unlocked the front door to let them in. Jade's mom obviously heard them from the kitchen. "Was dance class canceled?" she called.

"No...." Jade called back. "We found

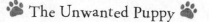

Bear! He ran off, Mom. We've got to call Jack's mom to come and get him." Quickly, she whisked her dancing tights off Bear's collar and stuffed them back into the bag. Her dad winked at her.

"Oh, my goodness...." Her mom appeared in the kitchen doorway. "Hello, sweetheart! What were you doing, running around on your own? Thank goodness you two found him before he went into the road," she added.

"I know. I didn't have my phone, though." Jade's dad walked into the kitchen and picked it up from the counter. "There's a cell phone number on his collar tag." He crouched down beside Bear, trying to read the tag and tap in the number while Bear licked his chin and tried to climb on top of him. "You silly dog…. Oh…. It's not ringing. It says that number is not in use."

Jade's mom frowned anxiously at Bear, who'd followed Jade into the kitchen. "Hmm…. Jack's dad has just changed jobs, so maybe that was an old work number. Now what are we going to do?"

"We could call school," Jade suggested, almost reluctantly. She didn't really want to help find a way to give Bear back. But Jack must be so worried about him. She could imagine how she would have felt if it were Honey.

"That's a good idea, sweetie, but I don't think anyone's in on Saturdays."

Mom sighed. "Oh! Are you hungry, puppy?"

Bear was sniffing hopefully at the edge of the table. He could obviously smell Jade's mom's half-eaten piece of toast.

Jade's mom eyed it, and then the dog. "No…. I'd better not send you home with bad habits. I bet you're not allowed to eat from the table." She went to the big kitchen cupboard and dug around in the back of it. "I thought so. I tried to throw it away a couple of times but it made me so sad…." She held up a bag of Honey's food.

Bear bounced and woofed excitedly as he heard the dog biscuits rattling in the bag, and he practically danced when Jade's dad found Honey's old bowl and they poured in a large helping. "After all," Jade's mom muttered, "we don't know when he got out. He might not have had breakfast."

"He doesn't look like he did," Jade said, giggling as Bear wolfed down the biscuits. "Here, you'd better have some water, too."

Bear finished the food and licked thoroughly around the bowl, obviously trying to make sure he hadn't missed any. Then he took a huge drink of water and sighed happily.

"He's so beautiful," Jade said as he came to nuzzle against her knees and began to lick her fingers. "If we can't find their number, can we keep him until school on Monday?" For a tiny moment she imagined keeping him forever—not telling Jack's mom and her family that they'd found him. But she knew it was only a silly daydream. "I bet they're really missing you," she whispered to Bear.

"I just realized something!" Mom brightened. "He might be microchipped. All we need to do is head down to the vet and get them to scan him—if he's microchipped, they'll have his address on the computer."

"Oh, yes." Jade stared down at her feet. Of course, that was the responsible thing to do....

Chapter Eight
The Best Day

Unfortunately, the phone number on Bear's microchip was the same out-of-date one that was on his collar. The vet had a backup number, a landline, but although it rang, there was no answer.

"I bet that's their old house number. But I don't understand why they wouldn't have updated all the details when they moved," Jade's dad said to the receptionist, shaking his head.

"It happens all the time," she told him. "You'd be amazed how many people just forget to do it. I'll call back and leave a message—even if it is their old house, the new owners might have their contact information."

Jade sat on one of the waiting-room chairs with Bear snuggled against her legs. She could tell that he didn't like the smell of the vet's office. His ears were all flattened down, and he was being very quiet and well behaved, as though he hoped no one would notice he was there. At least scanning his microchip hadn't looked as though it hurt.

"Yes, I suppose that's the best thing to do. Thanks for your help, anyway." Jade's dad sighed and came over to Jade and Bear. "Well, all we can do is leave a message. If they don't get back to us, we really will just have to take him to school on Monday. Poor Lauren! She must be frantic, wondering where he is."

Jade nodded, but she couldn't help thinking that it was a little bit Lauren and Ben's own fault. They should have bought Bear a new collar tag and made sure his microchip records were up-to-date.

"So what do we do now?" she asked.

Her dad shrugged. "We take him home with us and wait, I guess." He smiled at Jade. "And make sure he's well taken care of—I don't think that's going to be a problem, is it?"

Bear stood at one end of the yard, waving his tail uncertainly. Jade was running up and down the grass, tapping a ball between her feet. Was he allowed to join in? He'd tried to play with balls in the park before and been scolded and pulled away, but Jade was calling to him,

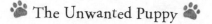

and the ball looked so tempting....

He crept forward, nosing cautiously at the ball, and Jade laughed. "Yes! That's it, keep going!" The ball rolled toward her, and she nudged it back over to Bear. "Come on! Yes!" she squeaked excitedly as he scratched and pounced at the ball with his front paws and it bounced off to the side. Bear watched eagerly, settling into a hunting crouch as Jade ran up to the ball again. This was a good game!

He chased the ball up and down the yard with Jade until he was worn out, and then flopped down in a patch of sun on the grass. He lay there happily, panting a little. Jade ran off into the house and Bear looked at the door, wondering if he should follow her. But then she came back out with a bowl of water for him to drink and lay down next to him. Bear drank the water greedily and then laid his nose down on his paws, sleepy in the sun. He could feel the warmth of her, lying next to his back, quiet and loving.

"Jade!"
Jade woke up with a jump. She hadn't

been sound asleep, just sleepy…. It was so warm for springtime, and there was something so special about lying there in the sun—especially when she was curled up with a dog.

Bear sat up, too, shaking his ears and snorting a little.

"I'm sorry, sweetie. Were you asleep?" Dad came walking across the yard.

"Only a little…."

"The people from Lauren's old house called back. They had her number, and I called her. I said we'd bring Bear back over—her husband's out looking for him, and she has the kids with her. Do you want to come?"

Jade chewed her lip. She sort of didn't—but at the same time, she wanted to stay with Bear for as long as possible.

"We can put Honey's old leash on him," Dad suggested. "It's still on the hook in the hall."

"Come on, Bear," Jade called sadly, trailing back into the house. He could tell that she wasn't happy, she thought, watching him follow her, ears down. "We have to give you back," she explained as she clipped on the leash and waited for Dad to find his keys, and Mom to grab a sweater. "I wish we could have kept you for longer...."

The walk back to Bear's real home seemed to take no time at all, even though Jade was trying to go as slowly as she could, and she thought Mom and Dad were, too. They stood outside Bear's house, looking doubtfully at the door, and Bear pressed himself against

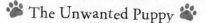

Jade's legs and whined.

"I don't think he wants to go back home," Jade said with a sniff. He didn't want to go, and she wanted to keep him. It was so unfair.

"He's probably just confused," Dad said gently, and he reached out to ring the bell.

Jade could hear footsteps and an excited voice—Jack. *He must be so glad that his dog is back*, Jade told herself, trying to block out her own feelings.

"You found him for us, Jade!" Jack squeaked, hugging her around the waist. "He ran out the door. He was so naughty."

"It's so lucky you found him," Jack's mom said. "Come in—have a cup of tea. It's the least I can do to say thank you."

"Oh, that's okay…," Jade's mom started to say, but Jack was already pulling Jade inside and into the kitchen.

Jack's mom hurried around, making drinks, and Jade watched as Bear sniffed thoughtfully at his basket and his food bowls.

"As soon as he ran off, I thought about his collar tag," Lauren explained, putting down cups of tea. "And then I realized we hadn't updated the microchip, either—I had such a long list of things to organize after the move."

"It's a tricky time," Jade's mom agreed. "So much to do."

Lauren sighed and looked over at Ben, who was getting cookies out of the cupboard. "In a way this has been a good thing, though. Losing Bear and realizing that we hadn't even remembered to buy him a new tag—it's made us see that we haven't been taking care of him properly."

She looked a little worriedly

at Jack, who'd run back into the yard where he was playing with his cars. Bear was standing by the door and watching him, but he didn't try to join in. "This morning we were talking about calling the lady we got him from and getting her to take him back. We've realized we just can't handle him, and it's only going to get worse as he gets bigger. We did try to talk to Jack about it, but I'm not sure he really understands."

Jade's mom and dad both nodded, and Jade could hear her dad saying something about that being a sensible decision, but it was as though she was hearing him from a long way away. There was a strange sort of rushing noise in her ears,

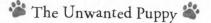

like she could hear her own heart beating. They were sending Bear back? She wouldn't even be able to see him in the park?

She wouldn't see him at all.

Her parents and Lauren and Ben went on chatting, but Jade sat silently, not even sipping the juice that Ben had poured for her. She was almost sure that if she moved at all, she would burst into tears. She couldn't look at Bear.

It seemed like hours until Mom said that they should get going. Jade stood up carefully, the way she did if she had a headache and sudden movements would hurt. It was all so wrong! When were they going to get rid of Bear? She hadn't even asked. She wasn't sure she could bear to know—but what if this was the last time she ever saw him?

Bear followed them down the hallway, and Ben held on tightly to his collar as Lauren opened the front door so he couldn't slip out again. Jade shoved her hands into the pockets of her jeans, in case she tried to push Ben's hand away and grab Bear's collar herself. The puppy was staring at her. His tail was tucked down, and his eyes looked so sad. He was unhappy, and he was going to be really confused when Lauren and Ben sent him back. Jade's own eyes filled with tears, and she turned away.

No one said very much as they walked along the street. Jade was concentrating on not letting her mom and dad see that she was crying. They'd think she was so silly—it wasn't as if Bear had ever been her dog. She knew that. He was just a friend, that's all.

"Jade, which would you like?" her mom said, and Jade realized that she must have been asked a question.

"Wh-what?" she asked in a wavery sort of voice.

"Would you like mashed potatoes or—Jade, what's the matter?" Her mom stopped and looked straight into her eyes. "Sweetheart, what is it?"

Her dad put his arm around her shoulders. "Oh, Jade, don't cry!"

"They're giving Bear back!" Jade wailed. She just couldn't hold it in any longer. "We won't even see him now."

"We did say we'd think about getting our own dog soon," Mom said gently. "Maybe even a Bernese mountain dog like Bear."

"I don't want another dog!" Jade looked up at her. "It won't be the same, don't you see?"

There was a moment of strange, waiting silence, and Jade looked up to see her mom and dad exchanging a thoughtful glance.

"You know," her dad said, "when they mentioned that they were going to give up Bear, I did wonder...."

Jade's mom shook her head. "So did I! But it just seemed a little odd to suggest we could take him!"

"You mean it?" Jade whispered.

Her mom laughed and looked at her dad. "Yes!"

Jade stared at them for a second more, and then she turned and raced back down the street.

Jade held up the treat—it was a piece of cheese. She'd discovered this was Bear's favorite after he'd eaten her packed-lunch sandwiches. Bear was sitting, just about—he kept half getting up and then sitting down again because he wanted the cheese—at the end of the line of boots that Jade had made.

"In and out! In and out, Bear!" Jade said hopefully, crossing her fingers. Bear eyed the cheese, and then the boots, and then marched straight down the side of the line instead of zigzagging through them like he was supposed to. Then he sat down in front of Jade, sitting beautifully, like the best-behaved dog ever. He stared up at her with huge, dark, hungry eyes, and she gave him the cheese anyway.

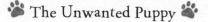

She couldn't resist those eyes and, after all, he *was* sitting.

"How's he doing?" her mom called from the kitchen. "Have you run out of cheese yet?"

"He almost did it," Jade called back. "And, um, yes. Can we have some more cheese, please?"

Bear turned to look hopefully toward the kitchen, too. He might not get this in and out thing, but he knew exactly what cheese was. He loved it almost as much as he loved Jade.

HOLLY WEBB

Holly Webb started out as a children's book editor, and wrote her first series for the publisher she worked for. She has been writing ever since, with more than 100 books to her name. Holly lives in England with her husband, three young sons, and several cats who are always nosing around when she is trying to type on her laptop.

For more information
about Holly Webb visit:

www.holly-webb.com
www.tigertalesbooks.com